Third Grade Ghouls

Third Grade Ghouls

Colleen O'Shaughnessy McKenna
Illustrated by Stephanie Roth

SCHOLASTIC INC.

New York   Toronto   London   Auckland   Sydney
Mexico City   New Delhi   Hong Kong   Buenos Aires

ISBN 0-439-56711-4

Published by Scholastic Inc., 557 Broadway, New York, NY 10012,
by arrangement with Holiday House, Inc.
SCHOLASTIC and associated logos are trademarks
and/or registered trademarks of Scholastic Inc.

12 11 10 9 8 7 6 5 4 3 2 1   3 4 5 6 7 8/0

Printed in the U.S.A.   40

First Scholastic printing, October 2003

To the real Gordon Barr and his wonderful family,
and to the handsome Mr. Schmidt and his bride
Winnifred from Put-in-Bay, Ohio.

C. O. M.

To Andy Aquino, Mahalo

S. R.

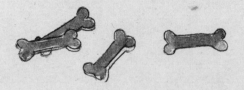

Third Grade Ghouls

Chapter
1

Gordie followed his brother, Doug, onto the school bus. Doug headed for the back of the bus where the fifth- and sixth-graders sat. Gordie slid into his favorite seat behind the bus driver. He waved into the mirror. The bus driver winked at him. Three stops later, Gordie slid over to make room for Lamont Hayes, his best friend. Lamont was carrying a very large black trash bag.

"Hey, aren't you supposed to leave the trash at the curb, Lamont?" asked Gordie. "This isn't a garbage truck."

Lamont laughed and stuffed the bag on the seat. "It's my Halloween costume. My mom is afraid my little sister will ruin it if it stays in the house."

"What is it?" Gordie tried to peek inside the bag.

"You'll see in a minute. Close your eyes, Gordie."

Gordie heard the trash bag rustling, then Lamont groaning as if he were trying to squeeze into a hole.

"Ready?" asked Gordie.

"Okay." Lamont's voice sounded as if he were under a pile of leaves.

Gordie opened his eyes and stared at Lamont's huge cereal-box head. Lamont's dark eyes peered out from the middle of a bowl of cornflakes.

"You're a box of cereal?" asked Gordie. He laughed. "That's so cool."

The box nodded. "My mom went to the Shop-For-A-Lot warehouse last week. I've been eating a *lot* of cornflakes."

"Your mom thinks up good costumes, Lamont." Last year Mrs. Hayes had tied green beach balls all over Lamont. He won their second-grade's Best Costume prize for being the best bunch of grapes.

Gordie hadn't had time to think of a costume yet. Usually Mom told him to go find something in the closet, or go as a ghost. "Does your mom have an extra box for me?"

"Sure," said Lamont. "She has a huge box for you. It's bigger than mine!"

"Great!" Maybe Gordie would have a chance to win first prize in the Halloween parade at school. Their classmate Lucy Diaz said her dad would donate ten free movie passes to the winner. Mr. Diaz owned Cinema World and was always giving away free passes. Gordie shared a locker with Lucy, but she never gave him anything but a hard time.

"I'll bring the box over after school," Lamont promised.

"Thanks, Lamont. What's on my box? Spaghetti?"

Spaghetti would be a great costume. He could spray-paint some tennis balls brown and pretend they were meatballs. Even the fifth-graders would clap when he walked by in the parade. Even Lumpy Labriola, who never clapped for anyone.

Lamont leaned closer. "Well, it's a big box of . . ."

"Sugar Pops?"

"Not exactly. We had to eat all the corn-flakes up first, and . . ."

"So tell me, Lamont."

"Toilet paper."

"Toilet paper?" Gordie screamed.

The bus driver glared at him in the mirror.

"Hey, Lamont," shouted Doug from the back of the bus. "Great costume. I always knew you were a little flaky."

Lamont grinned and twisted in his seat. "Yeah, and I'm real *corny,* too." He elbowed Gordie. "Your brother is so funny."

Gordie slumped into his seat. Doug

wouldn't think toilet paper was funny.

"Hey, cereal-box head," hollered Lumpy. "Is there a prize inside your box?"

Lots of kids laughed. Gordie and Lamont didn't laugh. Nobody wanted a big fifth-grader like Lumpy making fun of him. It was a good thing that Lumpy hadn't heard about the toilet paper.

"So, what are you going to be for the parade, Gordie?" Lumpy yelled. "Are you going to be a ghost *again?*"

"That old Lumpy," muttered Gordie. He had only been a ghost two times. Well, maybe three times, but so what?

"Lumpy doesn't know everything," whispered Lamont. He swung around and frowned at Lumpy. "He's not going to be a ghost this year."

Lumpy frowned back. "Oh, yeah? What's shrimp-face going to be then?"

"A giant box of toilet paper, that's what," Lamont called back. "Sixty-four rolls!"

The whole bus started to laugh. Even the

bus driver. Gordie covered his ears.

"Sorry, Gordie," said Lamont. He tapped Gordie's shoulder. "I didn't know everyone would laugh."

"Of course they would laugh. Who wants to be toilet paper? Lumpy will probably try to flush me down the toilet."

"Doug won't let him," said Lamont.

"Doug can't be with me all the time," said Gordie. "I'm going to have to think of a costume so scary that even Lumpy Labriola will scream. A monster maybe. A monster with seven eyes."

Lamont smiled. "Great. Paint your nails black. Paint your teeth black, too."

"And I'll smear yellow mustard on my teeth." Gordie felt much better. Things would be perfect once he got his costume ready. He'd be a huge, hairy, yellow-fanged monster. Lumpy would leave him alone and Gordie would end up winning first prize for being third-grade's greatest ghoul.

When the bus pulled up in front of the

school, Lumpy rushed past the other kids and poked Gordie on the arm. "I'll be watching for you, Mr. Toilet Paper. The judges are going to give you a prize for the worst costume."

Gordie watched Lumpy leave the bus. Could he scare Lumpy? Maybe Gordie should be a ghost again this year. At least he could hide under the sheet.

Chapter

2

Gordie flew off the bus and raced down the hall, even though there was a hall monitor by the water fountain. Who cared if he got a demerit? Everyone was going to make fun of him for the rest of the year anyway. He just had to find a scary costume. Maybe he could borrow Nana's fur coat. It looked like a giant raccoon.

"Gordie, wait up," cried Lamont. He held out his trash bag. "Here, you can be the cereal box for the parade."

Gordie shook his head. "No, that's okay. I'll think of something."

"Trying to scare Lumpy is like trying to

scare King Kong." Lamont sighed. "Hey, my mom bought a lot of shampoo, too. Maybe you could wear that box."

"I told the whole bus I was going to be scary. There's nothing scary about shampoo. Not even dandruff shampoo. I have to scare Lumpy."

Lamont grinned. "Good luck. Lumpy isn't afraid of anything."

Gordie opened his locker. "Maybe I could be a spider. One with twenty legs."

"Spiders only have eight legs," Lamont said.

"Then I'll be a double spider with lots of hairy legs."

Lamont tried to shove his cereal box inside his locker. "You better ask Miss Tingle if you're allowed to mess up science facts."

"She won't care." Miss Tingle was the best teacher in the school. She loved everyone in room 9 and she never got mad. If she almost got mad, she just flashed the lights on and off.

Gordie followed Lamont into the classroom. Miss Tingle was stapling paper pumpkins on the bulletin board. Maybe she could give Gordie an idea for a scary costume.

"Hi, Miss Tingle," said Gordie. "I was wondering if . . ."

"Beep, beep!" Lucy Diaz bumped into Gordie as she hurried past. She was carrying an armload of clothes.

"Hey, this isn't a Laundromat!" said Lamont.

"What do you have there, Lucy?" asked Miss Tingle.

"Clothes from my brothers' closets. I thought some kids could use them for Halloween costumes." Lucy dumped the clothes on her desk.

Gordie walked over to Lucy's desk. She had four older brothers who played a lot of different sports. Maybe he could get an idea for his costume from her stuff.

"I can be a football player, or a skier, or a hockey player." Lucy picked up a snor-

kel. "Or, a deep-sea diver who looks for treasures."

"How about a snorkel diver who plays football with sharks?" asked Gordie.

"Very funny, Gordie Barr. So, what are you going to be?"

"Gordie's going to be a box of toilet paper," said Mikey. "Sixty-four rolls."

"That's not true, Mikey," said Gordie. "Lamont was kidding. My real costume is a secret. It's going to be really scary."

"Don't be a ghost again, Gordie." Lucy tossed him a football jersey. "You can wear this."

"Football players aren't scary," said Gordie.

Miss Tingle flashed the lights on and off. "Take your seats, people."

Lucy grabbed the jersey back from Gordie. "You won't be needing this since you're going to be a big box of toilet paper."

"No, I'm not. I'm going to be so scary, you won't even be able to look at me." Gordie sank into his seat. "I'll be the scariest kid in the parade. Every kid in this school will have six nightmares because I'll be the gigantic ghoul of the school."

Lucy laughed. "If you can scare me, I'll give you five movie passes."

"Deal!" cried Lamont. He reached over and shook her hand.

"Wait," said Gordie. He didn't want to make a deal with Lucy.

Lucy stuck out her hand. "Shake on this, Gordie."

"No."

"I'm his agent, Lucy. I already shook on it for him. Gordie's going to scare every hair off your head."

Gordie sank into his seat. Was Lamont nuts?

The first bell rang and Miss Tingle clapped her hands twice. "Take your seats, children, and get out your spelling books."

Gordie opened his desk and grabbed his spelling book. He already knew all the words for the spelling test. He was ready for that. Too bad he wasn't ready for the Halloween parade.

Chapter
3

Gordie was glad third-graders didn't eat lunch with fifth-graders. He didn't want to hear Lumpy telling the whole cafeteria that Gordie had the dumbest Halloween costume in the world.

Lamont raised his hand. "Miss Tingle, can I go to the rest room? My pen leaked all over me." After Miss Tingle nodded, Lamont handed Gordie his lunch bag. "I have six peanut butter cookies in there, Gordie. You can have four since I made the bus laugh at you."

Gordie didn't think he could even eat one. Lumpy had chased his appetite away. Gordie followed room 9 down the stairs and into the noisy cafeteria. He ducked down behind Lorraine Morris. She had so much red fluffy hair that it hid Gordie.

When Lamont came into the lunchroom, he slid onto the bench near Gordie. "Is Doug going trick-or-treating with us tomorrow night?"

Gordie took a bite of his sandwich and shrugged. "I hope so. Nobody steals our candy bags when Doug is with us. But Lumpy keeps saying that only *babies* dress up and beg for candy. Doug said he probably wouldn't go."

"Lumpy is always causing trouble," said Lamont.

"I am never, ever going to stop trick-or-treating," said Gordie.

Lamont put four cookies in front of Gordie. "I have some windup teeth you can have tomorrow. Use them to scare Lucy."

"I'm not afraid of fake teeth." Lucy set her lunch tray down between Gordie and Lamont. "I'm not afraid of anything." Lucy laughed. "I'm not even afraid of Lumpy Labriola. Remember last Halloween when he rolled you down the hill, Gordie?"

Gordie sighed. Of course he remembered. His whole class laughed at him until Miss McPeak made them all stop. "Yeah. The sheet is still all grass-stained."

"That Lumpy," said Lamont. "He thinks he is so tough and cool."

"He's as big as my brother Ronnie," said Lucy. "And Ronnie is fifteen!"

Lamont lowered his voice. "Lumpy's mom is pretty tall, too."

Gordie glanced over at Mrs. Labriola. She was taller than the principal, Mr. Frattaroli. She was nice, except when a kid tried to take two milks. Or when someone tried to throw away a whole lunch. Maybe that's why Lumpy was so big. Maybe he was never allowed to throw away anything. Not even a pea.

"Lumpy is afraid of Ronnie, Gordie. You can dress up in his football uniform. He's number eight," said Lucy.

"Ronnie is a good player, but no thanks, Lucy," said Gordie.

"Ronnie burps a lot, but he's nice to me most of the time."

Lamont rolled a plum down the table to Gordie. "When does Gordie get the five movie passes, Lucy? He wants to take me this Saturday."

Lucy pointed a pretzel stick at Gordie. "When this kid scares me, which is never."

"I'll scare you," said Gordie. "Just don't run home and tell your brothers to chase me to Ohio."

Lucy laughed. "Okay. I promised you five passes if you scare me. What are you going to give me if you *don't?*"

Gordie held up a peanut butter cookie. "A cookie?"

"A cookie isn't good enough," said Lucy.

"What if Gordie comes to your house and bakes them himself?" asked Lamont.

"No way, Lamont!" said Gordie. Why was Lamont always opening his mouth and getting him into trouble?

Lucy narrowed her eyes. "It's a deal. Can my friends watch?"

"I don't know how to make cookies," said Gordie.

"You don't know how to scare me, either." Lucy took a long sip from her milk. "Do you have your own apron?" Lucy got up. "I have to go tell Madeline."

"Sorry, Gordie," said Lamont. He took a

huge bite of his sandwich. Then he took another bite. He was chewing very fast, as if he were in a sandwich-eating contest.

Gordie watched Lucy telling Madeline that Gordie couldn't scare a mosquito.

"Why did you tell Lucy I would bake her cookies?" said Gordie.

Lamont let his sandwich drop with a thunk. "I didn't think Lucy would take me seriously, Gordie."

Gordie crumpled up his lunch bag. "I have to win the bet so Lumpy and Lucy will leave me alone. I need a very scary costume by tomorrow."

"Go to the library and get on the computer," said Lamont. "Click on to ghouls.com."

"We don't have library until Monday. I'll just ask someone who is actually scary which costume they would wear in the parade."

Lamont laughed. "Good idea. Just find the scariest, meanest guy in the whole school."

"Yeah," said Gordie. He was starting to

feel better now. At least he had a plan. "So, who is the meanest, rudest, scariest guy we know?"

"Hey, Ma! I need you to sign this!"

Gordie's head flew up as if he'd been zapped. It was Lumpy, walking across the cafeteria to his mom.

"My teacher said I didn't study. But I did, right, Ma?"

Mrs. Labriola glared at Lumpy. Then she grabbed the paper and glared at him some more.

"He's your guy," whispered Lamont.

Gordie watched Lumpy and his mom. They were both about six feet tall. Their faces were getting redder and redder as they talked. Finally, Mrs. Labriola shook her finger in Lumpy's face and he walked away.

"I don't know which one to pick," said Gordie. "Both of the Labriolas are kind of scary."

Lamont pointed to Mrs. Labriola. "Better pick her. She won't roll you down a hill."

Gordie stood up and grabbed his lunch

bag. "Okay, Lamont, I'm going to toss my bag in the trash can. Then, I'll go over to Mrs. Labriola and say, 'Hi. If you wanted to think of the scariest thing in the world, what would it be?'"

Lamont laughed. "I know what she'll say."

"What?"

"Lumpy."

Chapter

4

"I'm not going to be Lumpy Labriola for Halloween."

Lamont was laughing so hard the whole table was watching him.

Gordie elbowed Lamont. "Come on, Lamont. Stop laughing. Lumpy's mom is going to come over here any minute."

"She's *your* mom now!" Lamont laid his head on the table and laughed some more.

Mikey walked over from his table. "What's so funny?"

"Nothing, Mikey," Gordie said quickly. "Lamont was just . . . just choking."

Lamont sat up. "I feel better now."

Gordie sighed. He never got mad at

Lamont. But if he did, he'd be mad now. "I'm going outside."

Lamont shoved the last bite of his sandwich in his mouth and stood up. "Me, too."

Gordie hurried to throw away his lunch bag. He turned toward the plastic bin and bumped into a little kid who almost dropped his tray. The boy's apple rolled across the floor and rested against Mrs. Labriola's shoe.

Mrs. Labriola picked up the apple. "You

should be eating this apple, not playing with it."

Gordie watched the little boy pick up a hot dog.

"It's too dirty to eat now," said Lamont.

Mrs. Labriola frowned. "You didn't eat very much lunch. What's your name?"

Gordie froze. Mrs. Labriola was acting like a cop about to give a speeding ticket.

"My name's Timmy. I can't eat 'cause two of my teeth are all wiggly." He opened his mouth and pointed to his front teeth.

Mrs. Labriola bent down and looked. "Oh, I see. I remember when Lumpy lost his baby teeth."

Gordie blinked. It was hard to imagine Lumpy with baby *anything*.

"I want to take the hot dog home to my dog." Timmy shoved the hot dog into his pocket. "He won't care that it's dirty."

Mrs. Labriola took Timmy's hand. "Let's wrap it up, Timmy."

"Do you like dogs?" Timmy asked.

Mrs. Labriola nodded. "I love dogs. But Lumpy is terrified of dogs."

Gordie smiled. Lumpy was afraid of dogs! Great! That meant Gordie didn't have to be a yellow-fanged monster. He could be a huge, yellow-fanged *dog* for Halloween.

Once Mrs. Labriola and Timmy left, Gordie grabbed Lamont's arm. "I can't believe it."

"I bet we're the only kids in school who know this secret."

"It's a top secret, Lamont."

"What's a top secret?" asked Lucy. She dumped her leftovers in the plastic bin and put her tray on the stack. "Tell me."

"No way," said Lamont. "Telling you something is like putting it on the radio."

"Come on. I'll give you a free movie pass, Lamont. You don't even have to scare me."

Gordie got worried. Lamont loved going to the movies. "We're not going to tell you, Lucy. Not even for a hundred movie passes, right, Lamont?"

"Ten passes," said Lucy. "And a tub of popcorn."

Gordie chewed his lip. Lamont loved movies and buttered popcorn. If Lucy threw in some Junior Mints, Lamont would tell her anything.

"It's a private secret, Lucy," said Gordie. "We'd be kicked out of school if we told you."

"Gordie!" cried Lamont. "Why would they kick us out of school because Lumpy's afraid of dogs?"

Lucy laughed. "Lumpy is afraid of dogs?"

"Lamont!" shouted Gordie. "You have such a big mouth!"

"Sorry!" Lamont slapped his hand over his mouth.

"Lumpy is too big to be afraid of dogs," said Lucy. "Dogs should be afraid of him."

"You're right, Lucy. Lamont was joking," said Gordie. "We were just kidding. The real secret is that"—Gordie looked around the cafeteria, searching for an idea—"that tomorrow is taco day. You can eat all the tacos you want, right, Lamont?"

"Yeah," said Lamont. "So wear your bib, Lucy."

Gordie and Lamont hurried to the stairs.

Lucy followed them. "Very funny. Lamont was telling the truth. Lumpy is a big, fat scaredy-cat."

Gordie was just filing up the steps when he stopped. He stopped so fast, Lucy slammed into him.

Gordie couldn't move. Standing in front of him was Lumpy Labriola.

"What did you say?" snapped Lumpy. "I'm not afraid of anything, Diaz."

"Don't call me Diaz or I'll tell my brothers, Lumpy." Lucy didn't look a bit scared.

Gordie took a few steps back. "Want to go outside, Lamont?"

"Who said I was a scaredy-cat? Name one thing I'm afraid of."

Lucy stared at Lumpy. Then she barked.

Lumpy's face flushed red. "Who said I was afraid of dogs?"

"Gordie said it was a big secret," said Lucy.

Gordie wanted to tell Lumpy that he hadn't said a word. But Lamont looked worried. Two fifth-graders walked past Lumpy and laughed. A tall kid with glasses tapped Lumpy on the shoulder and barked.

"Be quiet," snapped Lumpy. He turned and grabbed Gordie's shoulder. "Your big mouth just got you in a lot of trouble, toilet paper man. Big trouble." Lumpy turned and stalked away.

Gordie wanted to call out, "Hey, it was Lamont's big mouth, not mine." But he didn't. Even though Lamont was a blabbermouth, he was still Gordie's best friend. There was no reason to get Lamont in trouble, too. Besides, Gordie was in enough trouble for them both.

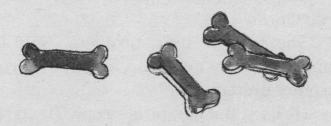

Chapter
5

Gordie tried to make himself as small as possible on the playground. He and Lamont stood near the playground monitor in case Lumpy was looking for them.

"Lumpy should be mad at Lucy, not me," said Gordie.

"She has four huge brothers," said Lamont. "Nobody gets mad at her. Will your brother protect you?"

"He'll try. But Lumpy is strong. Doug saw Lumpy pick up a motorcycle once."

"So why is he afraid of dogs, Gordie?"

Gordie shook his head. "Maybe a dog bit him when he was smaller."

"Hey, Gordie!"

Doug raced across the playground. Gordie and Lamont hurried over to meet him.

"Gordie, why did you tell everyone Lumpy is afraid of dogs?" asked Doug. "He's pretty mad right now."

"Mrs. Labriola told us Lumpy is terrified of dogs," said Lamont. "Then Lucy came over and forced us to tell her."

"You told Lucy Diaz a secret?" asked Doug. "Are you nuts, Gordie?"

"I'm the one who told her," said Lamont. "It just kind of slipped out."

Gordie nodded. "Yeah, Lucy wormed it out of him. She's the one who barked at Lumpy."

Doug lowered his voice. "I told Lumpy that he wasn't allowed to beat you up."

"Thanks, Doug," said Gordie. "Are kids still barking at Lumpy?"

"Not so much anymore. Who wants to get Lumpy mad?"

Gordie nodded. He didn't.

"Listen, Gordie, I have to go take a make-up test in my homeroom."

"Can I come?"

Doug smiled. "No. You guys will be okay. Stay by the playground monitor."

Gordie and Lamont stood by the monitor until Miss Tingle came out to take room 9 back inside.

"Lamont, make sure you tell Lucy not to tell anyone else the secret," said Gordie.

"Okay. Are you still going to work on your scary costume?"

"I have to. I don't want Lumpy to make fun of me and I don't want to lose the bet to Lucy." Gordie followed his class into the school and walked down the hall. He pulled off his jacket and headed for his locker. Maybe he should ask Lucy to bring in pictures of her big brothers. Gordie would tape them all over the front of the locker to remind Lumpy that Gordie shared a locker with Lucy.

"You'll be able to relax tomorrow night."

Lamont tossed his jacket into his locker. "We're going to have so much fun trick-or-treating."

Gordie smiled. Yeah, things would be okay. He'd ask Doug to help him make a big mask to wear with his scary costume. Lucy would scream her head off and Lumpy wouldn't know who was inside the costume.

Gordie opened his locker. A roll of toilet paper bounced off his head. "Yikes!"

Lamont laughed. "Here's your costume."

"Stop laughing, Lamont." Gordie leaned against his locker. "I bet Lumpy did this."

Mikey and Joey laughed.

"Halloween isn't until tomorrow, toilet paper man," said Joey.

"You're not a bit funny, Joey," said Lamont. "Just wait until tomorrow when Gordie wins first prize for having the scariest costume."

Joey just laughed harder and walked into room 9.

"They think they're so funny," muttered

Gordie. "Should I tell Miss Tingle about Lumpy putting toilet paper in my locker?"

"You don't know that he did it," said Lamont. "Maybe someone did it as a joke. Lucy likes jokes."

"Lucy wouldn't mess up our locker. It's hers, too." Gordie opened his locker again and ducked. He didn't want another roll of toilet paper to bounce off his head. He placed the roll on the bottom of his locker.

Gordie didn't think the toilet paper was a joke. Jokes were supposed to be funny and make you laugh. Gordie didn't feel like laughing right now.

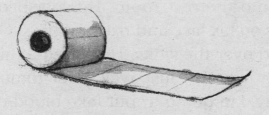

Chapter

6

"Recess is over, boys," Miss Tingle called from the door. "Time to come in."

When Gordie walked into room 9, Miss Tingle stopped him. "Gordie, are you okay? Your face is beet red. Why don't you go down to the rest room and splash cold water on your face?"

Gordie walked back out into the empty hall. He was glad to be alone. Gordie hurried into the rest room. He splashed cold water on his face and tried to think. Gordie leaned over the sinks. He stared at himself in the mirror. "Just wait until tomorrow, Lumpy. I'm going to put fake blood on my mask. I'm going to super-glue a fork on the top of my head. I'm going to scare everyone in the parade. Even the teachers will scream."

"No, don't!"

Gordie spun around. Someone was screaming already.

"Who's in here?" Only one stall door was closed. Little blue shoes were behind the door.

"I hate Halloween," cried a shaky voice. "Don't scare me."

"Don't you like all the candy you get on Halloween?"

The stall door opened and Timmy, the little boy from the cafeteria, walked out.

"I don't like monsters. I don't like witches." Timmy turned on the water and washed his hands. "I don't like pirates with swords, either."

"Do you like ghosts?"

Timmy shook his head. "No. Last year a real big ghost chased me with some chains." Timmy lowered his voice. "Then I threw up all over my teacher."

"I remember that. You're Larry Green's little brother." Gordie remembered how embarrassed Larry was when Timmy threw up. Larry yelled at him and said he was a big baby. Gordie knew Doug would never yell at him for throwing up.

"Larry said I better not throw up this year or else." Timmy wiped his wet hands on his jeans. He looked up at Gordie. "Don't be a monster with a fork in your head. When everyone screams, I'll throw up."

Gordie felt bad for Timmy. Last year the whole parade stopped when he threw up.

Someone pounded on the restroom door. "Gordie, time to line up for gym."

Timmy reached out and grabbed Gordie's arm. "Don't be a monster. Be a pumpkin."

"A pumpkin?" Third-graders weren't pumpkins. "Sorry, Timmy. I have to be a monster."

"Can I hold your hand then? Larry won't let me hold his hand."

Gordie frowned. Only first-graders held

hands. He opened the door. "I don't think third-graders are allowed to hold hands, Timmy. But I'll show you my costume tomorrow before the parade. Then you'll know that it's only me, okay?"

Timmy shook his head and stared at the floor.

"Timmy, I have to go to gym. I'll talk to you tomorrow."

"I won't be scared if you hold my hand."

Gordie sighed. Monsters didn't hold hands.

Timmy followed Gordie out into the hall. "Larry said if I throw up again, he is going to eat all my Halloween candy. I'll only have apples left."

Gordie knew Larry would do it, too. Larry Green ate everyone's leftover food at lunch.

Gordie hurried to get in line with his class. "Timmy, why don't you just stay home tomorrow and not see any costumes?"

Timmy shook his head. "I can't. My mom made me a dog suit. With a tail. She said it took a million hours to make it. I have to wear it, or else."

Or else? Moms always meant it when they said that.

Mrs. Bell opened the door to room 3 and motioned for Timmy. "Story time, Timmy."

"And you'll hold my hand, right, Gordie?"

"Wrong!" said Gordie.

"Please?"

Gordie took a deep breath. "Okay, you can hold my hand, but only if you get really scared." Gordie knew Mrs. Bell would make all the first-graders stay together so she wouldn't lose anyone. Gordie would be with the third-graders. The scariest ghoul in the school was not going to be stuck holding hands with a dog.

Chapter
7

The bus ride home seemed very long. Gordie and Lamont kept waiting for Lumpy to say something. But he never did. In fact, he walked right past Gordie and Lamont's seat.

"I bet he isn't the one who put toilet paper in your locker," said Lamont. "He doesn't look guilty."

"Lumpy always looks like Lumpy," said Gordie. "I hope I can find a monster costume if I can't borrow Nana's fur coat."

"Cool. You could smear ketchup in spots. Kids will think you were in a big fight with another monster."

Gordie thought his costume sounded better already. He could color a bag and cut out two holes for the eyes. He'd be Gordie, the monster. "Oh, no," said Gordie. He groaned. "Timmy Green wants me to hold his hand so he won't be scared during the parade."

"Tell him Miss Tingle said no. Then you're off the hook."

Lamont grabbed his book bag and stood up.

"But I . . ." Gordie had promised Timmy. It's true he didn't want to hold hands with a first-grader, but promises were important.

Lamont got off first. He turned and waved to Gordie at the door. "Ask Doug to find you something for the parade."

Gordie nodded. He'd have to do that. He was fresh out of ideas.

After the bus dropped them off, Gordie walked over to his brother.

"Doug, can you help me make a monster costume? Scary, but not too scary."

Doug smiled. "You can't be *too* scary, Gordie."

"I don't want Timmy Green to throw up. I told him I wouldn't scare him."

"How can you be a monster if you promised not to scare Timmy? That doesn't make sense, Gordie."

"I know. And Nana wouldn't like Timmy throwing up on her fur coat."

Scratch came bounding down the sidewalk. He had a gardening glove in his mouth. Gordie bent down and let Scratch run him over.

"Hi, boy." Gordie laughed as Scratch held him down with two huge paws. "You sure are lucky to be a dog."

"Hey, shrimp, go as a dog tomorrow."

"Not scary enough." Gordie didn't want to tell Doug that Timmy was going to be a dog. It would look dumb to have a big dog and a little dog holding hands. It would look like a dog date.

Scratch licked Gordie's face before he started barking and tore across the neighbor's yard.

"I hope Mrs. Cillo's cat can fly," said Doug.

Gordie got up and brushed himself off. "Are dogs afraid of cats?"

"No way." Doug pointed to Scratch who was tearing through Mr. Yurcon's flower bed. "Dogs *think* they are much braver than cats."

Gordie nodded as Scratch chased a fat yellow cat through Mr. Yurcon's mums. "I know! I'll be a cat." Gordie followed Doug up the driveway. "How do you like that idea?"

"But there's nothing scary about a cat," said Doug. "You told the whole bus you were going to be scary."

Gordie dropped his backpack by the side door. Why had he opened his big mouth on the bus?

"What if I were a wild black cat? You

could tell Lumpy and the other fifth-graders that I have rabies. Tell them the pound put me on their Ten Most Wanted list."

Doug held the side door open. "You're nuts, shrimp. But it may work. I'll tell them that you've never been declawed. At least you won't have to sweat to death wearing Nana's fur coat."

"Are you going to dress up for the parade?"

"Maybe," said Doug. "I may not, though."

"Can Lamont and I go trick-or-treating with you?"

"Fifth grade is too old to trick or treat."

Gordie sat down on the bottom step. If Doug didn't go trick or treating with him, Halloween night wouldn't be as much fun. Too bad this Halloween was off to such a crummy start.

Chapter
8

The next morning, Gordie hurried through breakfast. He rushed back to his bedroom and packed his Halloween costume. He folded a black sweatshirt, black sweatpants, and a black winter ski cap. He picked up the ski cap, pulled it on, and turned around to look in the mirror. He looked like a cat or a robber. Gordie raced down into the kitchen and found two twisty ties. He pulled up two corners of the ski cap and made two stubby ears.

Doug looked up from his cereal. "Where are your whiskers, Gordie? A cat has to have whiskers."

Gordie ran back upstairs and found his mother. "Can I take that pencil you use to make fake eyebrows?"

Mrs. Barr's eyebrows went up. *"What?"*

Gordie reached on her dresser and picked up a thin pencil. "This thing. Can I take it to school and use it for cat whiskers?"

"Just don't tell everyone I have fake eyebrows, okay?"

Gordie nodded. He wouldn't share one more secret about anyone.

Gordie added the pencil to his costume bag.

"I need Scratch's leash," said Gordie.

Scratch jumped up from the rug and raced to Gordie, wagging his tail.

"Sorry, boy. I can't take you on a walk right now. I need to borrow your leash for another dog. *A scared dog.*"

Gordie shoved the leash into his costume bag and sighed. Timmy was a scared dog, but Gordie was a scaredy-cat.

Ten minutes later, Doug and Gordie ran for the bus. The bus driver was dressed up as a pirate.

"Hurry up with you, lads," the bus pirate said with a smile. "Next time you're late, you'll be walking the plank, mates!"

Gordie slid into the seat behind the driver, trying to relax. At the next stop Lumpy got on. He was wearing a football jersey. He looked like a high school player. Gordie stared straight ahead.

"How are you doing, Lumpy?" asked the bus driver.

"Okay, Mr. Schmidt. How are you?"

"Can't complain, mate. Now, stow your gear and step to the back of me ship."

Lumpy laughed and Gordie saw the bus driver smiling in the mirror. Gordie couldn't believe Lumpy knew the bus driver's name. Gordie had been sitting behind the bus driver for years and never knew his name. He was just the bus driver.

By the time Lamont got on the bus, it was

pretty noisy. Mr. Schmidt had sent around a pumpkin filled with peppermints. Some fourth-grade girls were trying to get a song going, but everyone ignored them and kept trying to get more candy.

Lamont slid into the seat beside Gordie. "Sounds like a party in here. Did you get a costume, or are you going as the scary Gordie Barr?"

Gordie held up the plastic bag. "I have a costume."

"Is it scary?" Lamont swung around to look at the fifth-graders at the back of the bus. "I mean, is it fifth-grade scary?"

Gordie shrugged. "It's scarier than toilet paper. I hope it's scary enough so the fifth-graders won't boo me. But not so scary it will make Timmy throw up."

Lamont smiled. "Today's going to be fun. I hope I win the prize."

Gordie stared out the bus window. He didn't care about prizes. He just wanted the Halloween parade to be over.

When the bus reached the school, Gordie and Lamont bolted for the door. The principal was dressed up as a race car driver. He wore goggles and passed out candy corn from a silver trophy.

Gordie didn't want to wait in line for the candy corn. Lamont followed him down the hall. Gordie opened his locker slowly. Nothing fell out and hit him on the head.

Lamont stuck his head inside Gordie's locker. "Good. I don't hear anything ticking."

Gordie saw Lucy's costume hanging on a hook. It was pink and fluffy. It didn't look like Ronnie's football uniform. Gordie checked both shelves. Maybe Lumpy was tired of playing jokes on him. Good. Gordie tossed his costume bag in the locker. It hit Lucy's fluffy dress and the dress fell to the floor.

"Yikes," said Gordie. Lucy's costume probably cost a hundred bucks. Maybe two hundred. He bent and picked it up. He shook it off. Lucy would never know.

Gordie and Lamont walked into room 9. Miss Tingle was dressed as a Christmas elf. As soon as she saw Gordie she walked over and put her hand on his shoulder.

"Mrs. Bell told me you offered to take care of Timmy Green during the parade today."

Gordie nodded, then shook his head. "I was going to ask you. I know the first-graders have to stick together and the third-graders have to stick together, too."

"Timmy can walk with the third-graders." When she bent down to hug him, the bell on her cap jingled. "I'm proud of you."

Gordie smiled. This was the first time Miss Tingle had hugged him. She smelled good, like flowery soap.

"I would have offered to help Timmy," said Lamont, "but Gordie beat me to it."

Miss Tingle laughed. "Maybe you can help Timmy next year. He really is afraid of the costumes."

Gordie liked being hugged, but he still

didn't want to hold Timmy's hand.

"Why don't you go down to Mrs. Bell's room now, Gordie? Tell her to drop Timmy off when it's time for the parade. You can be in charge of him from there."

Gordie nodded. He had never been in charge of anyone before. Except Scratch, and that was usually at Thanksgiving when Gordie had to make sure the dog didn't eat the turkey before Nana arrived.

When Gordie walked into room 3, little first-graders were all over the place. There were clowns, princesses, lots of ghosts and cowboys, and even a red tomato with a green pointed hat for a stem. As soon as Timmy saw Gordie, he raced across the room and grabbed his hand.

Gordie pulled his hand away. He didn't want to start holding hands right away.

"Thank you so much for offering to take care of Timmy," said Mrs. Bell. "I'll drop him off before we line up."

"Look at me," said Timmy. Timmy twirled around. He looked like a real dog. He even had a collar on. That would be a perfect place for Gordie to hook the leash. If Gordie led Timmy by the leash, he wouldn't have to hold his hand.

"Look, Gordie." Timmy held a large dog biscuit in each hand. "My mom said to carry these."

Good, thought Gordie. If Timmy's hands

were filled he wouldn't try to hold Gordie's.

"I have something for you, too," said Gordie. "I brought a real dog's leash. I'll snap it to your collar when the parade starts so we won't get separated, okay?"

Timmy grinned. "We'll be side by side."

Just then a pirate and a ghost started chasing the tomato around the room. Mrs. Bell clapped her hands and started yelling at them. Gordie missed Miss Tingle all of a sudden. He wanted to get back to room 9.

"See you later, Timmy." Gordie headed for the door.

"Don't forget me," called Timmy.

Gordie nodded. He couldn't forget about Timmy and the parade, no matter how hard he tried.

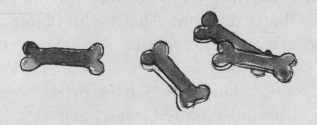

Chapter
9

Miss Tingle cancelled the math quiz right after lunch. Room 9 cheered.

"Thank you, Miss Tingle," called out Lucy. "My crown is scratching my head too much to think."

"What are you suppose to be, anyway?" asked Lamont. "The Queen of Aluminum Foil?"

Lucy swung around so fast her pointed silver crown flew off her head. "I am the Statue of Liberty, Lamont. That's a lot better than being a box of cereal that doesn't even have a prize in it."

Lamont laughed. "*I'm* the prize!"

Everyone laughed, even Lucy.

"Get into your costumes as fast as you can, class," said Miss Tingle. "If you need to change, go to the rest rooms, but no running in the hall."

Gordie looked at the clock. The parade would start as soon as the fifth-graders finished eating lunch. The whole school had to be in the parade, even if you didn't dress up. Everyone walked around the playground two times. The judges were a few parents and two bus drivers. They would decide who received the ribbon and the movie passes. Mr. Frattaroli would lead the parade.

"Too bad I can't win," said Lucy.

"You don't need to win," said Lamont. "Your dad owns Cinema World."

"I don't want the movie passes. I want the ribbon. I want the judges to call my name so people will clap."

Lamont clapped twice. "There."

Gordie put his costume bag on his desk and pulled out the sweatpants. He pulled them on over his jeans. Then he pulled the black sweatshirt over his head. He was about to look for the eyebrow pencil when he smelled chocolate. Larry Green was standing so close to Gordie that Gordie could see chocolate crumbs on his chin.

"Hi, Larry," said Gordie. "What are you doing in room 9?"

"I told Miss Tingle I wanted to talk to you. Timmy said you were going to walk with him in the parade."

"He asked me to." Gordie wished Larry

would walk with his own brother. "The costumes scare him."

"He acts like a baby sometimes. Just make sure he doesn't throw up. Or else!"

Before Gordie could think of something to say, Larry was gone.

Gordie looked over at Lamont, who was trying to pull a tablecloth over his head. A plastic cereal bowl was pinned to the cloth. He looked like a walking table. Gordie hoped Lamont would win first prize.

Lucy tapped Gordie on the shoulder. "What are you supposed to be? A bank robber with funny ears?"

"No. But I'm not finished, Lucy." Gordie reached inside his bag. Once he put his whiskers on, he'd look great.

Lamont came over, carrying his cereal box. "I'll put my box head on last so I can see." He took the eyebrow pencil from Gordie. "Here, let me do it. I'm going to give you a few scars with stitches, too. Then you can be a scary alley cat that fights all the time."

"I'll be back," promised Lucy. "So far you aren't very scary, Gordie. You're going to lose that bet to me."

"Don't listen to her," said Lamont. "You look great."

"Hurry up and finish getting ready," said Miss Tingle. "The parade is about to start."

Lucy walked over with bright red lips. She had added big hoop earrings and a flashing button that said: VOTE.

"The Statue of Liberty doesn't wear lipstick," said Gordie.

"Yes she does. For parades, she always gets dressed up." Lucy studied Gordie. "What are you? Whatever you are, I'm still not scared."

"Be nice, Lucy," warned Miss Tingle. "Gordie is a very scary-looking cat."

Lucy walked around Gordie. "Where's your tail?"

"A wolf bit it off," said Gordie. "Then I chased the wolf all the way to Chicago. I'm a one-of-a-kind karate cat." Gordie hopped

up and chopped his hands in the air.

Lucy pointed to Vanessa and Dana. "There are already two other cats in room 9, Gordie. You're not a scary cat. You're a *copy*cat."

"Go sit down, Lucy," said Miss Tingle. She patted Gordie on the shoulder. "You look great. Your costume won't scare Timmy. That is very kind of you, Gordie. I think kind cats are the best."

Gordie felt better. His costume was okay. At least Miss Tingle liked it.

"Timmy's here!" called Miss Tingle.

Gordie picked up the leash. Two times around the playground and the parade would be over. Next year, when Gordie was in fourth grade, he was definitely going to stay home on Halloween.

Chapter
10

The bell rang and classroom doors opened. Dozens of ghosts, pirates, clowns, princesses, and football players poured into the hall. Many teachers were dressed up in costumes and everyone was smiling. Gordie knew he'd smile only when the parade was finally over. He stood on his tiptoes and peered down to the fourth-grade home-rooms. He spotted two scary-looking witches and a tall kid wearing a green rubber mask. The mask was covered with bumps and warts. The eyeballs bounced up and down from springs.

Oh, no, thought Gordie. The moment Timmy saw the green monster, he'd turn green himself, and then . . .

"I have my dog biscuits," said Timmy. "I'm all ready."

"Good." Gordie snapped the leash on Timmy's collar. "All these kids are just kids, dressed up. Okay?" He turned Timmy around as the green monster walked by to get a drink from the fountain.

Miss Tingle smiled at Gordie and Timmy. "Would you two like to lead the line?"

"Yes!" cried Timmy.

"No, thanks," Gordie said quickly. "We're better off in the back." With any luck, the fourth-graders would file out after the fifth-graders. Timmy might not even see the witches and green monster.

"Remember, Timmy, if you get scared, close your eyes."

"But I can still hold your hand if I get real scared, right?"

"Right. But try not to get real scared."

"Our line is ready to move," said Miss Tingle. "Have fun outside."

Timmy gripped Gordie's arm. "That witch just waved to me."

Gordie turned around and stared at the tall witch with curly blond hair. "That's not a witch. It's really Mrs. Gerideau, the art teacher. Wave back."

Timmy gave a small wave. He was still clutching Gordie's arm. "Where are her teeth, Gordie? My art teacher has teeth."

Gordie smiled. "She just put black wax on her teeth. It's a Halloween trick."

"Maybe next year I will be a dog with no teeth," said Timmy. He let go of Gordie's arm.

Once they were outside, Timmy only closed his eyes twice. The first time was because a fifth-grade teacher blasted his whistle at a kid who wouldn't stop burping on purpose. The second time was when a skeleton rattled his rusty chains at Timmy.

"The skeleton is really Norton Lewis, Timmy. He always wears those orange sneakers," explained Gordie.

Lamont bumped into Gordie with his cereal box. "Sorry, Gordie. I can't see very well inside this box."

"Lamont's under the box of cereal, Timmy," said Gordie.

"I'm not afraid of *cereal!*" said Timmy.

As they neared the judges, Timmy waved his dog biscuits up and down. "I'm a dog with two bones," he called out.

A bus driver judge waved back. "A cat walking a dog. Very clever."

Gordie smiled. Clever was almost as good as scary.

"I don't have fleas," shouted Timmy.

The judges laughed. Then they wrote something on their clipboards. Gordie liked being a cat. He licked a fake paw. He had never thought about winning, but maybe he would.

Gordie looked across the circle and spotted the fifth-graders. It was easy to find them. Gordie just looked for Lumpy, who

seemed taller than ever in his football helmet and shoulder pads. Doug was behind Lumpy. He waved his baseball cap at Gordie.

"One more time around the circle, Timmy," Gordie said.

"This is fun," said Timmy.

When they were halfway around the second loop, someone screamed. Then the gym teacher blasted his whistle and raced across the playground, waving his hands. Gordie looked up and saw a huge golden dog galloping toward the parade.

Timmy pressed his face into Gordie's stomach.

"Remain calm, children," shouted Mr. Frattaroli. He clapped his hands, but the dog didn't listen to him.

The gym teacher chased the dog toward the swings. The dog barked from behind the slide. As soon as the gym teacher got close to the dog, he took off again. He barked and ran from one side of the playground to the other.

"I don't like big dogs." Timmy pressed his face harder into Gordie's stomach.

Lucy took off her crown and scrunched it up in a ball. She threw it at the dog. "That dog has a foamy mouth," shrieked Lucy. "He has rabies."

Lots of kids started screaming. Mrs. Gerideau told Lucy to be quiet.

Gordie put his hand on Timmy's back. He stared at the dog that was racing around the fifth-graders. Some of the fourth- and fifth-graders broke out of line and chased the dog. Gordie knew he had seen the dog before somewhere. He didn't look mean. Just hot and excited that so many kids wanted to play with him.

"What's going on?" Lamont asked. "I can't see a thing."

"A dog is chasing everyone," said Gordie.

"Where's Lumpy?" asked Lamont. "Is he hiding in a tree?"

Lumpy! Gordie searched the crowd. He saw the janitor holding a piece of rope, trying to get the dog to come to him. Gordie saw Doug, down on one knee and waving the dog to him. But where was Lumpy?

"That dog is nuts!"

Gordie jumped. Lumpy was standing near him, out of breath and looking scared under his football helmet.

"I'm going inside," muttered Lumpy. He turned to go.

"Where do you think you're going?" asked Lucy. "You're not supposed to be with third-graders."

"Be quiet, Lucy," said Gordie. He looked past Lucy and saw an old man at the edge of the playground. Suddenly, Gordie knew where he had seen the dog before. It was at the vet's office last week when they took Scratch for shots. The dog's name was Randy and he lived near the school.

"I know that dog," said Gordie. He unsnapped the leash from Timmy. "He's a nice dog. He's just scared."

"I'm scared, too," said Timmy. "I don't feel so good."

Lumpy was staring at the dog. "How can you tell he's scared?"

"Because his tail is between his legs," said Gordie. "See how low to the ground it is?"

Lumpy squinted in the sun.

Timmy let the dog biscuits drop. "I feel sick," he said.

"This is no time to throw up, Timmy. We have to get that dog or he may run into the road and get hit by a car."

Lumpy picked up a dog bone. "Give the dog a bone."

"We have to get him, first." Gordie dropped the leash and walked slowly toward the dog. "Randy!"

"Get back in line, Gordie," said Miss Tingle. "Stay away from the dog."

"I know him," said Gordie. He took another step closer and yelled. "Randy!"

Randy's head jerked up. He stared at Gordie, his tail beginning to wag slowly.

Gordie knelt and patted the ground. He held out the bone. "Here, Randy. Come here, boy."

The dog walked slowly toward Gordie, his tail wagging faster.

"Get away from the dog," yelled the gym teacher. "Get that kid away from the dog."

Randy stopped, his head dropped. Gordie turned around. "Lumpy, give me the leash."

Lumpy took a few steps toward the dog and then stopped.

A few fifth-graders barked from the other side of the circle.

"He's a good dog, Lumpy," Gordie whispered.

Lumpy took another step. Timmy was now holding on to Gordie's leg.

Randy sat down, his tongue hanging out. Gordie stood up and took a slow step backwards. "Give me the leash, Lumpy."

Lumpy took a small step and handed Gordie the leash. Gordie remembered how much Scratch loved his leash. Whenever he saw it he knew he was going for a walk. Gordie held up the leash and the dog raced toward him.

"He's a good dog," Gordie reminded Lumpy and Timmy. "Here, Randy."

The dog ran over and sat down in front of Gordie. He looked up at the leash and barked once.

Gordie snapped on the leash and patted Randy on the head. "Good boy."

"Way to go, shrimp," called Doug. He clapped three times. Then lots of kids started to clap.

Gordie smiled. Timmy smiled back and tossed a dog bone near the dog. Randy bent down and gently picked up the bone. He held it in his mouth like a tiny cigar.

Gordie whispered to Lumpy. "That's his owner coming across the playground. Want to take the dog over?"

Lumpy shook his head. From across the circle came a few more barks. Lumpy glared, then chewed on his lip. Gordie heard a few kids from the fourth grade start to laugh. Randy flopped down and put his head on his paws.

"That's okay. I'll do it," said Gordie.

Before Gordie could take a step, Lumpy took the leash.

"Come on, Randy."

Randy scrambled to his feet, his tail wagging. Gordie saw how pale Lumpy looked under the helmet. But he kept walking. Gordie watched him walk across the middle of the circle and hand the leash to the old man. The man patted his dog and then shook hands with Lumpy.

"Nice job, Lumpy," Doug called.

A few kids clapped again. No one barked.

The parade started up again. When the line stopped moving, the judges gave the blue ribbon to a giant Hershey Kiss. They gave her an envelope with the movie passes inside. Everyone clapped. The Hershey Kiss was too wrapped up in foil to take the envelope, so the second-grade teacher took it and everyone clapped some more. Mr. Frattaroli thanked everyone for coming. He thanked Lumpy for returning the dog. Then the parade was over.

Lamont pulled the cereal box from his head. "Gordie, you should have gotten the prize. You got the dog to come to you, not Lumpy."

"Yeah," said Timmy. "You weren't scared a bit."

"That's okay. Mr. Frattaroli didn't see that part. He was busy yelling at the fifth-graders."

"You should have gotten a hundred movie passes for being braver than Lumpy." Lamont slapped Gordie a high-five.

Miss Tingle gathered room 9 around her. "You did a nice job, children." She smiled at Gordie. "Gordie, you were very brave. You took care of Timmy and the dog."

"He's a hero cat," said Lamont.

"But he's not very scary," said Lucy. As she walked past him to stand next to Miss Tingle, she smiled. "You don't have to bake me cookies, Gordie. I was only kidding."

"You were?"

"Yeah," said Lucy. "But you don't get any free passes. Better luck next year at the parade."

Gordie wasn't sure he wanted to think about next year's parade. He and Lamont followed their class inside. Mrs. Bell and the first-graders were waiting by the clock for Timmy.

"Thanks, Gordie," said Mrs. Bell.

Timmy smiled. "Thanks. Now Larry won't eat my candy."

Gordie glanced up at the clock. It was almost time for dismissal. Once it got dark, it would be time to trick-or-treat. Maybe Lamont's mom could walk around with them.

Gordie pulled off his ski cap and opened his locker. Nothing fell out. "I guess Lumpy ran out of toilet paper."

Lamont shoved his cereal box inside his locker. "Lumpy didn't put the toilet paper in your locker." His voice sounded funny.

"How do you know?"

Lamont closed his locker. He wouldn't look at Gordie. "Because I did."

"What?"

Lamont shrugged. "I was just trying to be funny. I thought you'd laugh and then I was going to tell you. But you didn't laugh. You got mad and I was afraid you'd stop being my best friend."

"I thought Lumpy did it."

"I know. Sorry." Lamont scratched his head. "When I was trying to get the ink off my hands I saw the toilet paper. That's when I thought of the joke."

Gordie closed his locker. "Maybe if I hadn't been scared about Lumpy it would have been funny. A *little* funny."

Lamont nodded. "It was a weak joke."

"It's okay. You can't be really funny *all* the time."

Lucy stomped to their locker and threw her pink fuzzy dress inside. "That dress is too itchy. I'm going to be a ghost tonight."

Lamont and Gordie laughed. Gordie looked up and saw Doug walking down the hall.

"Hey, shrimp. Nice work out there." Doug high-fived Gordie. "Lumpy's been bragging about catching the dog."

"Not true," said Lamont. "Gordie did it all."

"Lumpy did a good job, too," said Gordie. He knew Lumpy didn't want to walk the dog over to the owner. But he did.

Lamont hurried down to get a drink.

Doug grinned. "Lumpy was bragging, but he told me that you were kind of cool for a shrimpy third-grader."

Gordie laughed. Hearing that was better

than winning the ribbon or the passes. Maybe now Lumpy would leave him alone. "At least I won't have to worry about him stealing my candy bag tonight."

"He won't," said Doug. "I won't let him."

"You're going out with me? Trick-or-treating?" Gordie started to laugh. "Thanks, Doug."

Doug swatted Gordie's shoulder with his hat. "It will be fun. Tell Lamont to come over right after dinner. I heard about a house on Coral Drive that's giving out homemade popcorn balls."

Doug turned and hurried back down the hall. Gordie pulled off his sweatshirt and wiped the whiskers and fake scars from his face. He didn't need to be scary anymore. He could just be Gordie.

The bell rang and Gordie raced inside room 9. This Halloween night would be the best night of all. He didn't need to be a ghoul. He was one *cool* cat.